THE AMERICAN GIRLS

17  64

KAYA, an adventurous Nez Perce girl whose deep love for horses and respect for nature nourish her spirit

17  74

FELICITY, a spunky, spritely colonial girl, full of energy and independence

18  24

JOSEFINA, an Hispanic girl whose heart and hopes are as big as the New Mexico sky

18  54

KIRSTEN, a pioneer girl of strength and spirit who settles on the frontier

18  64

ADDY, a courageous girl determined to be free in the midst of the Civil War

19  04

SAMANTHA, a bright Victorian beauty, an orphan raised by her wealthy grandmother

19  34

KIT, a clever, resourceful girl facing the Great Depression with spirit and determination

19  44

MOLLY, who schemes and dreams on the home front during World War Two

1764

Kaya's Escape!

A Survival Story

By Janet Shaw

Illustrations Bill Farnsworth

Vignettes Susan McAliley

American Girl®

Published by Pleasant Company Publications

For information, address: Book Editor, Pleasant Company Publications, 8400 Fairway Place, P.O. Box 620998, Middleton, WI 53562.

Visit our Web site at **americangirl.com**

Printed in China.
02 03 04 05 06 07 08 LEO 12 11 10 9 8 7 6 5 4 3 2

PICTURE CREDITS
The following individuals and organizations have generously given permission to reprint images contained in "Looking Back":

pp. 66–67—Idaho State Historical Society 63-221-22, Jane Gay Collection (girls with play tepees); Northwest Museum of Arts & Culture/Eastern Washington State Historical Society, Spokane, WA (girls with cradleboards); pp. 68–69—Western History/Genealogy Dept., Denver Public Library (child on horse); Northwest Museum of Arts and Culture/Eastern Washington State Historical Society, Spokane, WA (elder with woven bag); pp. 70–71—Cumberland County Historical Society, Carlisle, PA (portrait of boarding school girl); Northwest Museum of Arts and Culture/Eastern Washington State Historical Society, Spokane, WA (cooking class); Lewiston Tribune, Lewiston, ID (girl weaving); Photo courtesy of Antonio Smith (language class).

Library of Congress Cataloging-in-Publication Data

Shaw, Janet Beeler, 1937–
Kaya's escape : a survival story / by Janet Shaw ;
illustrations, Bill Farnsworth ; vignettes, Susan McAliley.

p. cm. — (The American girls collection)

Summary: In the fall of 1764, after Kaya and her sister are kidnapped from their Nez Perce village by enemy horse raiders, she tries to find a way to escape back home. Includes historical notes on education and learning among the Nez Perce Indians.
ISBN 1-58485-426-X — ISBN 1-58485-425-1 (pbk.)
[1. Kidnapping—Fiction. 2. Escapes—Fiction. 3. Survival—Fiction. 4. Nez Perce Indians—Fiction. 5. Indians of North America—Northwest, Pacific—Fiction. 6. Northwest, Pacific—Fiction.]
I. Farnsworth, Bill, ill. II. McAliley, Susan, ill. III. Title.
PZ7.S53423 Kay 2002 [Fic]—dc21 2001036812

FOR MY DAUGHTER,
LAURA BEELER,
AND MY GRANDDAUGHTER,
MAYA RAIN BEELER BALASSA,
WITH LOVE

Kaya and her family are *Nimíipuu,* known today as Nez Perce Indians. They speak the Nez Perce language, so you'll see some Nez Perce words in this book. "Kaya" is short for the Nez Perce name *Kaya'aton'my',* which means "she who arranges rocks." You'll find the meanings and pronunciations of these and other Nez Perce words in the glossary on page 72.

Table of Contents

Kaya's Family

Toe-ta
Kaya's father, an expert horseman and wise village leader.

Eetsa
Kaya's mother, who is a good provider for her family and her village.

Kaya
An adventurous girl with a generous spirit.

Brown Deer
Kaya's sister, who is old enough to court.

Wing Feather and Sparrow
Kaya's mischievous twin brothers.

. . . and Friends

Kautsa
Kaya's grandmother on her mother's side.

Speaking Rain
A blind girl who lives with Kaya's family and is a sister to her.

Steps High
Kaya's beloved horse.

Two Hawks
A ragged and angry captive who becomes Kaya's friend.

CHAPTER
ONE

TAKEN CAPTIVE!

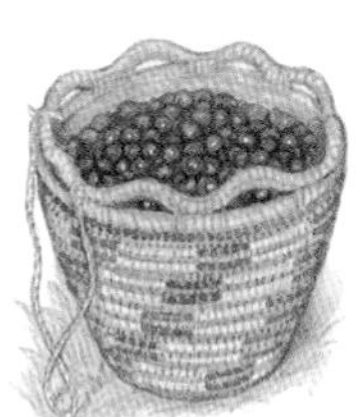

Kaya dug her fists into the sides of her waist and stretched. Her back was sore from bending over to pick huckleberries. Since first light, she and the other girls had moved along the hillside, plucking ripe berries from the bushes and dropping them into the baskets they wore at their waists. Now the sun was high overhead. It was time to sort and dry the berries they'd picked in the cooler hours. Kaya thought dried berries were good, but ripe ones were a feast. When she thought no one was looking, she sneaked a handful for herself.

"Look, Magpie's stealing berries!" Little Fawn cried. "If she eats too many now, we won't have enough when winter comes!" She gave Kaya a teasing grin.

Kaya winced. Not a single day went by without someone calling her by her awful nickname—Magpie. Earlier in the summer, while visiting her father's family in *Wallowa*, she'd gone off to race her horse when she was supposed to be taking care of her little brothers. Whipwoman had told Kaya she was no more responsible than a thieving magpie! When all the children were switched for Kaya's disobedience, they began calling her "Magpie." Each time Kaya heard that nickname, it stung like Whipwoman's switch!

It was now late summer, and Kaya was back in Salmon River Country, where her family had joined her mother's band of *Nimíipuu*. They had traveled upstream and set up camp to pick berries in the higher country. Her father and many of the other men had gone even farther into the mountains to scout the deer and elk trails. It was time for the hunt. Soon the men would bring back as much game as they could so that everyone would have plenty of meat for the winter. With the dried meat, fish, and berries, there would be good provisions for the cold season to come.

Kaya untied the basket from her belt and spread leaves over the berries to keep them from falling out of the basket. She set her basket with those her mother and her big sister, Brown Deer, had filled. All the women and girls had been berry picking. Even the youngest girls wore little baskets—though they were allowed to eat more berries than they saved.

Kaya's grandmother was loading baskets onto her horse. *Kautsa* glanced over her shoulder at Kaya, then nodded at a little girl with her tiny basket. "Remember when you were that young?" she asked Kaya. "Remember how you'd run to give me the first few berries you picked?"

Kaya smiled, glad to be reminded of those happy days. "I remember you always praised me for my berries," she said. "You said I'd be a good picker one day."

"And you are!" Kautsa said. She hung the last bags onto her saddle, then patted her horse. Leading it, she began to walk with the others down to the tepees set in the meadow near the stream.

Kaya walked alongside Kautsa, matching her

strides to her grandmother's long ones. Heat rose from the stony path and shimmered around her legs. "The sun's hot, isn't it?" she said.

"Aa-heh!" Kautsa agreed. "The day is hot and our work is hard. But we need to pick berries so we won't go hungry this winter."

Kaya studied the thick groves of lodgepole pines that ringed the meadow below. "Could Speaking Rain and I sleep outside the tepee tonight?" she asked. "I think we'd be cooler in the meadow."

"We'll be cool enough inside," Kautsa said. "I want you two near me. With many of our men away, we'll be safer if we stay close together. The boys are keeping the herd close by, too. Look, there's your horse with the others."

Kaya shaded her eyes. She quickly identified Steps High by the star on her forehead. Kaya's horse was grazing at the edge of the herd with some mares and their foals. Perhaps Steps High sensed Kaya's approach, for she lifted her head and whinnied.

Kautsa halted her horse. She picked some large leaves from a thimbleberry plant beside the trail, then sprinkled a pinch of dried roots on the earth in thanks for what she'd taken. She used the leaves to wipe sweat from Kaya's forehead and then to dry her own face. "Go sit in the shade with Speaking Rain for a little while," she said. "The heat has tired you."

Kaya found Speaking Rain sitting under a pine tree. Speaking Rain was blind, so she'd stayed in the camp with the elderly women and men. She was weaving a beargrass basket that Kautsa had begun for her.

"I brought you some huckleberries, Little Sister," Kaya said. She placed a handful of berries into Speaking Rain's outstretched hands. Since Speaking Rain's parents had died, she'd lived with Kaya's family and been a sister to her.

Kaya sat beside Speaking Rain in the shade of the pine tree. "Our dogs chased two black bears out of the berry bushes this morning," Kaya said.

"Everyone wants these berries," Speaking Rain said. She ate hers one by one, making them last as long as possible. As she munched, she tipped her head toward Kaya. "Why do you sound so sad?"

Kaya knew she couldn't hide anything from

Speaking Rain. Maybe because Speaking Rain couldn't see, she heard everything sharply. "Little Fawn caught me sneaking huckleberries," Kaya admitted with a sigh. "She called me Magpie again."

"I hope that nickname will fade soon," Speaking Rain said. Again she cocked her head, listening. "Isn't that your horse whinnying to you? Go to her. Nicknames don't mean a thing to a horse!"

Gratefully, Kaya squeezed Speaking Rain's hand—Speaking Rain always understood her.

As Kaya walked toward the herd, she whistled her horse to her side. Steps High rubbed her head against Kaya's shoulder. Her horse's muzzle was as soft as the finest buckskin. "Hello, beautiful one!" Kaya whispered against the horse's sleek neck. It always comforted Kaya to stroke her horse.

As Steps High nuzzled her, Kaya glanced back at the clearing where women spread the berries on tule mats to dry in the sun. She saw her two little brothers bouncing on a crooked cedar tree, pretending to ride a horse. Nearby, little girls played with their buckskin dolls. Dogs lolled beside the tepees, their tongues out. In the wide meadow, boys rode herd on the horses. Thin clouds drifted

toward the Bitterroot Mountains in the east. *Stay close to be safe*, Kautsa had reminded her. Kautsa was wise in these things, and Kaya had heard that warning all her life. But right now, this quiet valley seemed the safest place she could imagine.

"Listen!" Kautsa said in a low voice. "The dogs are growling! Wake up!"

Kaya tried to waken in the deep of night. She heard Kautsa's sharp command, but sleep was like a hand pushing her down. Nearby, some dogs growled, then began to bark fiercely. Kaya sat up and rubbed her eyes. What was wrong?

Her mother peeked out the door of the dark tepee, then ducked back inside. "Strangers in our camp!" *Eetsa* said. "Get dressed! Quick! Enemies!"

Enemies! Enemies in their camp! The warning was a jolt of lightning—swiftly Kaya was on her feet. Her heart pounding, she struggled into her dress. Kautsa, Brown Deer, and Speaking Rain were doing the same. They all tugged on their moccasins and crept out of the tepee. Kautsa pushed Speaking Rain and the twin boys ahead of her. Brown Deer picked up one of the little boys. Eetsa picked up the other one. "Follow me!" Eetsa whispered. "Kaya, take Speaking Rain to the woods! We'll hide there!" Crouching, Eetsa ran for the trees, Brown Deer and Kautsa right on her heels.

The moon was rising above the trees bordering the clearing. Kaya could see women, children, and old people hurrying from the tepees for safety in the woods. Some men ran toward the edge of the camp where dark figures ducked between the horses tethered there. Raiders! Enemy raiders! They'd slipped into camp hoping to make off with the best horses, but the dogs had given them away.

Kaya's mouth was dry with alarm. She clasped Speaking Rain's hand tightly. But instead of following Eetsa into the woods, as she'd been told, she went in the direction of the herd. Where was Steps High? Would raiders try to steal her horse?

Kaya saw the woman named Swan Circling head toward the horses, too. A raider was about to cut the rawhide line that tethered her fine horse. Swan Circling had as much courage as any warrior. She stabbed at the raider with her digging stick. She knocked him away from her horse, which reared and whinnied in panic.

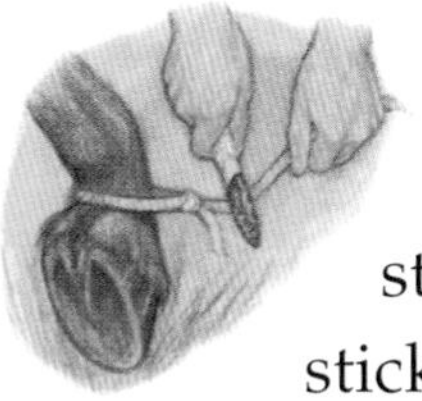

digging stick

The raider leaped onto the back of another horse he'd already cut loose. With a fierce cry, he swung the horse around and galloped straight through camp, coming right at Kaya and Speaking Rain!

With a gasp of fear, Kaya tried to run out of his way, pulling Speaking Rain behind her. Too late! Kaya threw herself onto her stomach, dragging Speaking Rain down with her. The raider jumped his horse over them and plunged on.

Kaya struggled to her knees. Now other raiders raced through the camp toward the herd. They lay low on their horses, trying to stampede the herd so no one could ride after them. The horses snorted and screamed with alarm. A few broke away. Was Steps High with them? Kaya whirled around. Nimíipuu men with bows and arrows were running to cut off the raiders.

Arrows hissed by. Kaya clasped Speaking Rain's hand again and ran for the safety of the woods. A horse brushed against her, almost knocking her down. She felt someone seize her hair, then grasp her arm. Speaking Rain's hand was yanked from hers. A raider swung Kaya roughly behind him onto his horse. She sank her teeth into his arm, but he broke her hold with a slap.

Kaya looked back for Speaking Rain. Another raider was dragging her onto his horse. "Speaking Rain!" Kaya cried, but her cry was lost in the tumult. The raiders raced after the herd, which ran full out now. The Nimíipuu men gave chase on foot, but they were quickly outdistanced.

Terrified, Kaya clung to the raider's back. The herd was thundering down the valley, the raiders in

Arrows hissed by. Kaya clasped Speaking Rain's hand again and ran for the safety of the woods.

the rear. The night was filled with boiling dust. Hoofbeats shook the ground and echoed in Kaya's chest. She caught a glimpse of Steps High running with the others. Her horse had been stolen by the enemies. She was their captive, too, and so was Speaking Rain. And it was Kaya's fault!

All that night, and on through the next day and night, the raiders ran the stolen horses eastward. When their mounts tired, they paused only briefly before jumping onto fresh horses and going on. Kaya knew they wanted to get out of Nimíipuu country before they were caught.

Because the raiders didn't rest, Kaya and Speaking Rain couldn't rest, either. The mountains and the valleys below went by in a blur. In her fatigue, Kaya sometimes thought she saw a blue lake in the sky. Sometimes she thought the distant, rolling hills were huge buffalo. And sometimes she did fall asleep, her head bumping the raider's back. He slapped her legs to waken her. She thought, then, about jumping off the running horse, but she knew she'd be injured or killed on the narrow, stony trail. *Maybe it would be better to die than to be a captive,* Kaya thought. But she couldn't abandon Speaking Rain.

When the sun was high overhead, the raiders finally stopped to rest. They left a scout to guard their trail and took the herd to a grassy spot by a little lake where the horses could feed and drink. Kaya saw Steps High standing by the water with the other foam-flecked horses. Their heads were down and their chests heaved from the punishing journey. How she wished she could go to her horse!

When the raiders gathered to share dried meat, Kaya got a better look at them. They were young, bold, and proud of themselves for stealing so many fine horses. She thought they spoke the language of enemies from Buffalo Country. Though Kaya couldn't understand their words, she knew that they boasted of their success. Perhaps they were proud, too, that they had driven the herd all the way through Nimíipuu country to the northern trail through the Bitterroot Mountains.

The raider who'd seized Speaking Rain offered her some of the buffalo meat. When she didn't respond, he waved his hand in front of her eyes, then made a noise of disgust. Kaya knew he was angry that the girl he'd captured for a slave was blind. He pushed her down beside Kaya and stalked back to the circle of men. Kaya held her close.

Speaking Rain leaned against Kaya's shoulder. "Where are we?" she whispered.

"Somewhere on the trail to Buffalo Country," Kaya whispered back. She put some of the food she'd been given into Speaking Rain's hand.

"What will happen to us?" Speaking Rain's voice quavered.

Though Kaya trembled with fatigue, she kept her voice steady. "Don't you remember what happened when enemies from the south stole some of our horses? Our father and the other warriors got ready for a raid. As the drummers beat the drums, all the women sang songs to send off our warriors with courage. Our warriors followed the enemies over the mountains and brought back all our horses! Our warriors will make a raid on these men, too. They'll take you and me back home with them. And they'll take back all of our horses, as well."

"Are you sure?" Speaking Rain murmured.

"Aa-heh!" Kaya whispered. "I'm sure."

But, in her heart, Kaya was far from certain.

Already they'd traveled a long way over the mountains. *Toe-ta* and the other men might not have returned to the berry-picking camp yet. When they did, the raiders might have already left the mountains and hidden themselves securely in the country to the east. What would happen to Kaya and Speaking Rain—and Steps High—then?

Kaya squeezed Speaking Rain's hand. "We have to be strong, Little Sister."

"Aa-heh," Speaking Rain agreed. "We'll be strong."

One of the raiders motioned for the girls to lie down. He tied Kaya's leg to Speaking Rain's with a length of rawhide so they couldn't run away. Lying huddled together, they softly prayed to *Hun-ya-wat*, asking for strength. Kaya was exhausted, but her head buzzed with fears. "I'm afraid to sleep," she whispered to Speaking Rain.

"Me, too," Speaking Rain whispered back. She put her cheek against Kaya's shoulder. "Remember the lullaby that Kautsa used to sing to us?"

Kaya nodded. Then, to her surprise, Speaking Rain began to sing gently, "*Ha no nee, ha no nee.* She's my precious one, my own dear little precious one."

Kaya glanced at the raiders—would they be angry at Speaking Rain's song? The men were lying down to rest. One glanced at Speaking Rain and shrugged as if he had nothing to fear from a lullaby.

Lulled by Speaking Rain's gentle voice, Kaya slept.

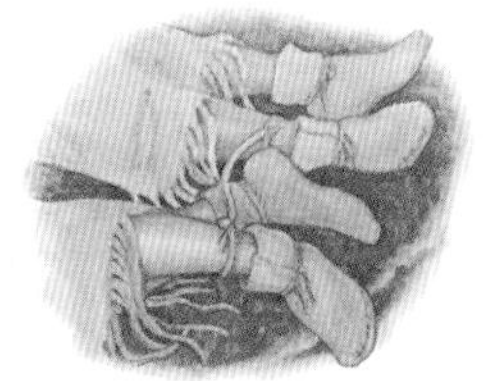

CHAPTER
TWO

SLAVES OF THE ENEMY

The raiders moved the herd eastward over the Buffalo Trail as quickly as they could. As they rode, Kaya caught glimpses of the Lochsa River in the valley, but the trail stayed on the top of the ridge. The going was easier up here than in the wooded gullies filled with windfall trees.

Kaya had been on this trail before. It was an old, old pathway made long before Nimíipuu had horses. In some places it split and braided together again where travelers had walked around fallen trees or boulders. In other places it was only a narrow ledge hugging a cliff. Kaya watched the horses carefully when they came to the dangerous ledges. Surely the raiders were pushing them too fast along this bad part of the trail. A horse that lost its footing would fall down the rocky slope and perhaps be killed.

The gentle old pack horse that belonged to Kautsa often stumbled in fatigue. Kaya kept her eye on the old horse, hoping he could keep up. But on a curving ledge, he slipped on the loose rocks. Kaya held back a cry as the old horse tumbled down the bluff in a shower of stones and lay still at the bottom. Wouldn't the raiders slow the other horses now? But no, they only pushed them faster. Kaya kept her gaze on Steps High and prayed that her horse would keep her footing. *Be strong!* she urged Steps High—and herself. Where were the enemies taking them?

Each night at last light, they camped in open glades where the horses could graze. A raider back-scouted the trail to see if they were followed. Kaya hoped that Toe-ta and other men were coming behind and would overpower the raiders. She thought that young men from Buffalo Country were no match for Nimíipuu men! But when the scout returned and the raiders continued on without rushing, Kaya knew no one was behind them.

At the highest point on the pass, Kaya gazed back at the mountains that loomed between her and her home country. Her courage sank low. She told herself that Hun-ya-wat had made the sky above her and the earth beneath her. *I am in His home no matter where I go,* she thought. Still, fear was a bitter taste in her mouth as they moved farther from her people.

Each night the raiders tied Kaya's leg to Speaking Rain's. At first light, the raiders untied them and sent Kaya to gather heavy loads of wood for the fire. They fed Kaya and Speaking Rain only the scraps from their meals. Kaya felt like the starving dogs that sometimes appeared at camp out of nowhere, cringing and groveling for a bite of food. She vowed that if she ever got back to her people again, she would never chase off those desperate, sad-eyed dogs.

When they passed some hot springs, where steaming water spouted from the rocks, the trail ran down the east side of the mountains. In another day they'd reached the broad river valley below. Kaya remembered passing this way with her family when they went to hunt buffalo on the plains beyond.

Then, this country had seemed full of promise and adventure. Now, it seemed strange and menacing. A wide, swift river flowed north, down the valley. If the raiders crossed the river, they'd be well on their way to their home country. How would she and her sister get home from so far away?

In this valley, the raiders moved the horses at night to avoid being seen. Shortly after first light they came to a small buffalo-hunting camp of their people, hidden in a canyon. The hide-covered tepees were decorated with animals and birds painted in brilliant colors, so different from the brown tule mat tepees of Kaya's people. As the raiders approached the camp, the hunters and the women gathered to greet them.

The raiders rode proudly through the camp, displaying the horses—and the girls—they'd stolen. Though Kaya wouldn't let her feelings show, she was sick to see the raiders praised and honored. She winced when the men looked over the horses and stroked the ones they liked best, Steps High among them. How she hated to have enemy hands on her horse!

All the men and women in the camp were pleased and smiling, except one dirty boy with a sullen face who stared grimly at Kaya. It came to her that the angry-looking boy was a slave, too, and that soon she and Speaking Rain would look as tired and bitter as he.

Kaya stared at her feet when the women came to inspect her and Speaking Rain. The women pinched the girls' arms to feel their muscles, then shook their heads and talked among themselves. They didn't sound pleased.

Kaya and Speaking Rain were dirty and their hair was tangled. They were used to bathing in the cold river and cleansing themselves in the heat of the sweat lodge every single day. Since they'd been captured, they hadn't been able to wash.

sweat lodge

When the women saw Speaking Rain's cloudy eyes, they frowned and spoke angrily to the raiders. Were they saying that a blind slave was nothing more than another belly to feed? Would they decide that Speaking Rain was no use to them and abandon her here, so far from Salmon River Country? But one raider took Speaking Rain's arm and led her to a young mother with a baby. He said something that caused the mother to look more kindly at Speaking Rain. Kaya guessed he'd told the mother that the blind girl wasn't entirely useless—she could sing lullabies and could help tend the baby while the mother worked. Kaya hoped they'd soon realize what a skilled cord maker and weaver Speaking Rain was, too.

One of the older women, with gray hair and a lined face, led Kaya to her tepee. Bold designs of otters were painted on the tepee in bright yellow and red. Kaya thought of the old woman as Otter Woman. She sat Kaya down and gave her buffalo meat to eat. When Kaya had eaten, the woman took Kaya to where other women were cleaning hides. She handed Kaya a sharp-edged rib bone and made a scraping motion. She wanted Kaya to scrape the fat and meat from a hide that was staked to the ground.

Kaya had often helped Kautsa clean hides. She knelt by the buffalo hide and began to scrape at it with the rib bone. Otter Woman watched her work for a little while, then nodded in satisfaction. Kaya scraped even harder, until her shoulders ached and her arms were sore—she vowed to work twice as hard in order to make up for Speaking Rain. Somehow she must protect her sister.

When night came, Otter Woman led Kaya and Speaking Rain into her tepee. She spread hides for them beside her sleeping place and motioned for them to lie down. Taking a thick rawhide thong, she tied it around Kaya's ankle and then around her own. She made the knots tight so Kaya couldn't untie the thong and run away. She didn't bother to tie up Speaking Rain—a blind girl wouldn't try to escape.

Speaking Rain pressed against Kaya's side. "Be strong," Kaya whispered to her.

Otter Woman gave her a sharp pinch that meant, *Hush! Go to sleep!*

Kaya clenched her teeth and vowed she would not cry, not even in the dark. But how could she sleep when her heart was aching so badly? She and Speaking Rain were slaves—they might never see their people again.

At first light, Kaya was sent to gather firewood. She watched the hunters ride away from camp to hunt buffalo in the valley. Later in the day, when the men returned with the buffalo they had killed, they gave the meat and hides to the women. Otter Woman set Kaya to work and led Speaking Rain to sing to the baby.

All day the women worked, cutting up the meat and hanging the strips on poles to dry. They scraped and tanned the hides, wasting nothing. Kaya's arms and back ached from the hard work of scraping. When she grew dizzy from the sun and weary from the work, she told herself to be strong for Speaking Rain.

Black-and-white magpies swooped over the drying meat, stealing bits for themselves. Magpie—Kaya's nickname. She had tried to be more responsible, but then she'd disobeyed Eetsa's order to run for safety in the woods.

That mistake had put her and Speaking Rain into captivity. *Maybe I deserve that nickname, after all,* Kaya thought miserably. She picked up a magpie feather and put it in the bag on her belt, a reminder that she *must* think of others before herself.

From where Kaya worked, she often caught glimpses of Steps High grazing with the other horses. If only she could get to her horse, touch her,

All day the women worked, cutting up the meat and hanging the strips on poles to dry. Kaya's arms and back ached from the hard work of scraping.

stroke her! Kaya watched for a chance to approach the herd, but the boys who tended the horses never seemed to leave them.

One evening, when the sun blazed on the horizon, Kaya saw a horse move away from the herd and come nearer to the camp. The horse was Steps High! The herders didn't seem to notice the lone horse, or maybe the sun blinded them when they looked her way. Kaya ran behind the tepees and into the sagebrush beyond the camp. She stopped there and whistled softly. Her horse raised her head and came closer.

Before Kaya could reach her horse, a man strode up beside her, a rawhide rope in his hand. Angrily, he struck Kaya's legs with the rope and gestured for her to get back to the camp. As she turned to go, she saw him put the rope bridle on Steps High's lower jaw. Confidently, he leaped onto Steps High's back and rode away from the camp.

Kaya watched her beautiful horse galloping swiftly across the plain. *If only I could jump on your back and race away from here!* she thought.

The man kicked Steps High until she was running flat out. Her shadow flew at her heels. Then she began to buck! The man whipped her with his quirt and sawed at the rope bridle in her mouth. He dragged the horse's head around and rode her in a circle.

When he managed to subdue her, he rode her back toward camp and whipped her harder. Blood stained the lather on her neck and shoulders.

Kaya wanted to cry out, *Stop!* But she could do nothing to protect her horse—she was a slave.

When Kaya was sent into the thickets to gather firewood, she sometimes took Speaking Rain along to help carry back the heavy bundles. The slave boy was sent for wood, too. Kaya thought he was about her age, and she wanted to know more about him. But when she came close, he frowned and turned away. Kaya knew he must be ashamed to be doing the work of women. Kaya didn't follow him—these times were her only chance to talk freely with Speaking Rain.

"The hunt will soon be over," Kaya said one

morning. "They have almost as much dried meat as the pack horses can carry."

"Aa-heh," Speaking Rain sighed. "It's getting colder, too. Soon they'll start back to their country."

"If only we could escape before they take us farther away," Kaya said.

"Aa-heh!" Speaking Rain agreed.

"But how can we?" Kaya asked. "We'd have to go when it's dark, and at night I'm tied to Otter Woman."

"Could you cut the thong?" Speaking Rain asked.

"The knife is in her pack, but I can't reach it," Kaya said.

"But I'm not tied up," Speaking Rain said. "I'll find the knife and give it to you."

"Aa-heh!" Kaya thought a moment as she wound a thong around the armful of dry branches that Speaking Rain held.

Speaking Rain was quiet, too. "Even if you cut yourself free, I'd never keep up with you on the run," she said slowly. "You'll have to go without me."

Kaya winced at the thought. "I'd never do that!" she said. She'd gotten her sister into this, and she couldn't leave her here as a slave.

"You *have* to leave me." Speaking Rain's voice was firm. "You must escape so you can bring others back to get me."

Kaya pressed her fingertips to Speaking Rain's lips. "Don't say that! How could I go without you?"

"Because it's our only hope," Speaking Rain said.

Kaya lifted a bundle of wood onto Speaking Rain's back and took the second bundle onto her own. "But even if I escaped, could I get to Salmon River Country before snow falls?" she asked.

Speaking Rain was quiet for a moment, thinking. "Could you take your horse?" she said. "You'd travel much faster on Steps High."

"They're sure to see me if I try that," Kaya said. "I'd have to slip away on foot. But if I go on foot—" Her head was spinning. "I don't know what to do. Help me."

"Think," Speaking Rain said. "If Kautsa were captured, what would she do?"

Kaya blinked. She knew the answer to that. "Kautsa would try to escape."

"Aa-heh," Speaking Rain said. "We must start

hiding some of our food for your journey."

As they trudged back to the camp, Kaya's mind raced with questions. *How can I leave my sister behind? What will happen to Steps High?*

Then a more terrifying thought came to Kaya: *What if I escape, but I'm captured again? What would the enemies from Buffalo Country do to me then?*

When Kaya came back to the camp from scraping hides that day, she saw the skinny slave boy tending a fire. There were burrs caught in his hair, and his only clothing was a ragged breechcloth and worn moccasins.

As she came near him, he motioned for her to stop. He glanced around, then with his hands he threw her the words, *Do you speak sign language?*

Kaya had learned how people talked with gestures when they couldn't speak each other's language. She answered with her hands, *I speak sign language.*

What tribe are you? he signed.

She pointed to herself, then swept her hand from her ear down across her chin. *I am Nimíipuu,*

her hands said. *What tribe are you?*

I am Salish, he signed. Then he ducked his head because others came near.

Kaya went on to the Otter tepee, but her thoughts were on the boy. Her people had many friends among the Salish. Nimíipuu often fished and traded with the Salish. Some had even married Salish men and women. Perhaps she and this boy could find a way to help each other.

The next time she had a chance, she picked up some sticks and took them to where the boy was building a fire. Placing the sticks by his feet, she crouched beside him. Would he frown and turn away again?

Instead, he met her gaze—maybe he, too, had been thinking they might help each other. She threw him the words, *What are you called?*

I am called Two Hawks, he signed.

She signed to him, *I am called Kaya.* "Kaya," she said out loud.

He narrowed his eyes and said slowly, "Kaya."

She nodded. Then she had an idea. Perhaps she and Two Hawks could escape together. Two would have a better chance to make it back to the Buffalo Trail and over the mountains than one traveling alone. Would he come with her?

And could she trust this boy? She wished she could know him better before she risked telling him her plan—he might betray her to the enemies in the hope of being rewarded with more food.

Kaya watched for a chance. It came when she and Two Hawks were sent to bring cooking water from the river.

When Kaya was sure no one could see them in the reeds by the river, she signed, *How long have you been a slave?*

I've been a slave for a long time, he answered. *I was captured in a raid on our village. I don't know where my family is, or even if anyone is alive.*

Kaya glanced over her shoulder. They were still alone, but it wouldn't be long before others came here for water. This could be the only chance she'd have to tell him her plan. She'd have to take the risk. *Pay attention to me!* she signed. *I'm going to go to Nimíipuu country. Soon. Come with me to my family!*

His dark eyes bored into her. Then he threw her the words, *I want to go to Nimíipuu country with you.*

Though his solemn expression gave away nothing, she realized he understood! *We will need hides. We will need food,* she signed.

He shook his head. *No! Let's go now!*

Kaya frowned. *This foolish boy!* she thought. If he acted recklessly, he'd put them both in danger. Didn't he know they'd have to wait for a dark night when they couldn't be seen? Didn't he realize they must plan ahead if they were to make it back safely? *Be patient!* she signed. *I'll give you a signal.*

Now! he repeated. Then he pointed to the horse herd not far downstream.

Kaya looked. Men were separating a few horses

from the herd. Other men were tying bundles of buffalo hides onto the backs of the horses. She saw that Steps High was one of the horses carrying a load of hides. *What are they doing with those horses?* she signed.

I understand their words a little, he signed. *They're going to trade those horses and hides to another hunting party. Then they'll leave for Buffalo Country. Soon! We must run away now!*

Kaya's mind was whirling—Steps High was going to be traded away! Even now the men were riding off with the loaded horses. Steps High tossed her head and whinnied. She trailed behind the others as if she knew she was being taken far away from Kaya.

Grief was a knife in Kaya's chest as she watched her beloved horse disappear over the rise. Two Hawks was right—they must escape soon or be taken much, much farther from home country.

Kaya bit her lip. How could she bear to leave her sister, and lose her horse as well?

Chapter Three
Escape!

Toward last light, the clouds turned red and the west wind blew more and more strongly. Kaya smelled the scent of rain in the wind. She heard small birds sing the high, whistling notes that meant a storm was on the way. By dark it would be raining hard, and everyone would stay inside the tepees with the door flaps closed. The storm would give her and Two Hawks a chance to escape.

When she saw lightning spike down from the clouds, she went to find him. He was banking the fires with ashes. She caught his eye and signaled to him, *Go! Tonight! Meet at the big tree!*

Soon rain lashed the tepees and thunder shook

the earth. The dogs huddled down with their heads buried in their tails. Everyone, except for a lone guard, gathered inside. Otter Woman tied Kaya's leg to hers and settled down under several hides to sleep out the storm.

Kaya waited until she was certain everyone slept soundly. Then she whispered in Speaking Rain's ear, "The knife—in the pack beside the door."

Kaya felt Speaking Rain slowly inching herself away from their sleeping place. If she made any sounds, the wail of the storm covered them. After what seemed a long time, Kaya felt Speaking Rain's hand on hers, then the knife in her palm. Gently, Kaya began to work the knife against the rawhide thong—there, she'd cut it! She forced herself to lie still a while longer to be sure Otter Woman hadn't felt anything.

At last, Kaya eased herself away. To deceive Otter Woman if she woke, Speaking Rain took Kaya's place beside her.

Quickly, quietly, Kaya dressed, slid the knife into her bag, and folded up a sleeping hide. She put the little bag of food they'd saved into her bundle, too. Then her courage almost failed her—how could she leave her sister? She clasped Speaking Rain's hand. Speaking Rain squeezed back. Their touch was a vow that they'd be together again. Kaya dragged herself on her stomach under the edge of the tepee until she was outside in the howling storm.

The camp was shrouded in darkness and the rain blew sideways. Kaya didn't see the guard—maybe he was checking on the horses. She crept, keeping low to the ground, until she left the tepees behind. Then she began to run as she had never run before. She sped, wet sagebrush stinging her legs, until she made out the big cottonwood towering over the woods. Was Two Hawks there? Had he been able to escape, too?

As Kaya skidded down the slope toward the big tree, she slipped. She was on her hands and knees when she heard Two Hawks call softly from the bushes, "Kaya?" Never had her name been more welcome to her!

She didn't see the boy until he was right in front of her. In a flash of lightning, she saw that he carried a bundle and wore leggings he must have stolen from a raider. He beckoned for Kaya to follow, then

In a flash of lightning, she saw Two Hawks.

started running across the open plain.

They ran westward into the wind. They had to cover as much ground as they could. As soon as it was light, the raiders would discover that their captives had run off. They'd follow swiftly on horseback. Kaya and Two Hawks must be well away and hidden by then.

All night they ran through lashing rain, but before first light the storm had passed over. Behind them the gray sky shimmered like an abalone shell. They ran along a rocky outcropping until they found a shallow opening beneath an overhang. Two Hawks dragged tumbleweeds over their tracks to cover their trail. Then they spread a hide under the rocky shelf, lay down on it, and covered themselves with the other hide. Two Hawks pulled a tumbleweed into the opening to shield them. Kaya thought she was too frightened to sleep, but in only a moment she fell into a black slumber.

A hand pressed over her mouth woke her. Who held her down? A raider? Then she realized it was Two Hawks signaling her not to speak or move. She heard distant hoofbeats, then the sound of horses running not far from where they lay. Scouts had followed them! Scarcely breathing, she pressed herself against the earth. The hoofbeats became fainter and disappeared. Kaya and Two Hawks had hidden themselves well. But would the scouts find them on their return? The boy must have been thinking the same thing. *Stay still!* he signaled to her.

All day they lay under the ledge. Slowly the light faded and night returned. The enemy scouts hadn't come back. Perhaps they'd given up their search, but there was no way to know. Kaya and the boy would have to be on the lookout every moment so they could see without being seen.

At last Two Hawks signaled to her, *Let's have a look around.* They crept out of their hiding place like prairie dogs out of a burrow. They ate some of their dried meat and sipped rainwater from a hollow in a stone. Then they made their way to the top of a low ridge and paused there to get their bearings. The moon seemed to float up out of the dark lake of waving prairie grasses. The stars were low and bright.

Kaya had been told many stories about the stars to help her find her way. She gazed up at the vast star-map shining above them. She saw the group of stars called the Seven Duck Sisters. But she concentrated on the star that never moves, the North Star, called Elder Brother. With Elder Brother as a guide, she calculated the way west.

Follow me! she signaled to Two Hawks. He shook his head. Again she motioned for him to follow her, but he stayed put. *Does he think I can't read the stars?* Kaya thought. She stamped impatiently and started walking. Before she'd gone more than a few steps, he came after her. Oh, she hoped she wouldn't lead them astray. If she made a mistake in her directions, they wouldn't be able to find the Buffalo Trail.

All night they walked into the wind, which was rising and getting colder. They were near the foothills now, but they would never be able to discover the Buffalo Trail in the dark. They would have to chance moving by day if they were to find it. But first they must rest for a while. When the morning star appeared, Kaya signed to Two Hawks, *We need a lean-to for shelter.*

Enemy scouts might still be looking for them, so Kaya chose a spot hidden deep in a thicket. With the knife, she cut several branches from a pine and leaned them together to make a frame. Then she cut an armful of thick, short branches.

Help me, she signed to Two Hawks.

His lips turned down and his eyes were slits. *Building a shelter is the work of women,* he signed. *I won't do the work of women anymore!*

Don't you want to get warm? Kaya signed. *Come on, help me.*

You work, Two Hawks signed. *I'll keep a lookout.* He turned his back on her.

Kaya wove branches into the frame until the shelter was completed. She crawled inside, with Two Hawks right behind her. There was room enough for them to sit upright and eat the last few bites of their food. Kaya chewed slowly. Her belly ached with hunger and her legs shook with fatigue. As they wrapped up in their hides, her mind was filled with worries. Would they manage to find the trail again? Could they cross the mountains before snow blocked the pass? In spite of her exhaustion, sleep was a long time coming.

Kaya woke to full sun and the sound of geese.

When she crawled out of the lean-to, the last grasshoppers of the season sprang up around her. Two Hawks stood grimly gazing up at the flock of geese flying south. Did he know their flight meant snow could be on the way?

Hunger made Kaya dizzy—surely Two Hawks was hungry, too. She pointed to the dark mass of the foothills ahead. She knew there would be fish in the streams running through the hills. *Let's get some fish,* she signed. *Follow me!*

Two Hawks glowered at her. *Men lead and women follow. You follow me!*

Kaya huffed in exasperation. But she decided not to fight with him—maybe he wouldn't be so disagreeable after they got something to eat.

Soon they were deep in the foothills. Kaya kept looking back, but she saw no signs of enemy scouts. Perhaps they were already on their way to their own country in the east. Before her, the Bitterroot Mountains seemed to reach up to the sky. Snow already lay on the highest ridges. Kaya clutched her hide around her shoulders and shivered. She and Two Hawks didn't have much time. But she was so tired and hungry that her legs wobbled. She needed food and water, and she needed rest. *We must stop here,* she signed.

Two Hawks frowned. *We must go on!*

I can't go on, she signed.

He looked at her hard, his jaw set. *We have to go on!* he signed. He walked off as if he didn't care whether she followed or not.

If this skinny boy can keep going, then so can I! Kaya thought. She caught up with him, but they made slow progress. The woods were full of windfall trees they had to climb over. Twigs tore at Kaya's face and arms, and often she stumbled and fell. Then she heard the sound of a stream. Was this the stream that led to the Buffalo Trail? *We'll rest here and fish tomorrow,* she signed.

Two Hawks turned to her with a sullen expression. *Don't tell me what to do. My father is a warrior. Someday I will be a warrior, too.*

Right now you're only a boy! she signed. *And I know better than you.*

You're not the leader, he signed. *I am! I say we go on!*

Anger flared in Kaya's chest. It had been her idea to escape. If it hadn't been for her, he'd still be a captive. She was the one who had gotten them this far. She knew they'd never make it home if they didn't guard their strength carefully. *I say we build a shelter and rest!* she signed.

Two Hawks screwed up his face in a scowl. *I am not your slave! I am no one's slave anymore! I do as I choose!* He turned on his heel and started running alongside the stream. In a moment he'd broken through some bushes and disappeared.

Kaya was so upset that her heart was beating like a drum. How could this boy be so foolish! Should she let him go on alone, or try to catch up with him again? She knew they'd be safer if they stayed together, whether he thought so or not—and she didn't want to face the night alone. So, against her will, she started plodding wearily upstream.

Kaya ducked under branches and climbed over rocks. When she smashed her head against a cedar limb, she went to her knees in pain. *Let him go on if he wants*, she thought. *I need to rest*. Crawling on her hands and knees, she started to move under the cedar tree to sleep.

Her hand touched something warm and furry. What was it? She pushed back the branches and looked. It was the body of a fawn that an animal had killed. She knew that cougars hunted elk and deer in these woods. This was a fresh kill—the cougar that had made the kill must be nearby. Surely it would come back for its meal. But if the cougar came upon a running boy, it might think that he was more prey and go after him.

Kaya's first thought was to get away from the kill and hide—let Two Hawks look after himself! Then she thought of the magpie feather in her bag. She'd kept that feather to remind herself that she must think of others before herself. She got to her feet and hurried upstream.

Around the bend she saw Two Hawks ahead of her on the pale, sandy shore. He was crouching at the edge of the stream, drinking from his cupped hands. When he heard her coming, he glanced her way. And as he did, she saw the flash of a cougar leaping down from an overhanging limb!

Chapter Four

On the Buffalo Trail

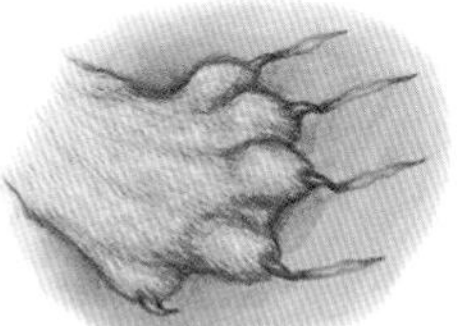

"Look out!" Kaya cried. Two Hawks spun onto his side, and the cougar landed on the sand beside him. Kaya ran splashing up the stream, shouting and flapping her deer hide at the cougar. It clawed and bit at Two Hawks's arms and shoulders. Kaya lunged forward and pounded her fist into the cougar's nose. With both hands, she grabbed handfuls of sand and threw them into the cat's eyes.

Blinking and snarling, the cougar released Two Hawks and began to back away. It was a thin, young cat with a lot of scars. Showing its teeth, it turned tail and retreated into the woods.

Two Hawks yanked off his deer hide. Kaya

motioned for him to let her see the wounds on his arms. She washed away the blood and exposed the scratches, which were not deep. The deer hide he wore—and Kaya's quick action—had saved him from deeper slashes.

Kaya knew how to stop the bleeding. Although it was almost last light now, she found the plant called *wapalwaapal*, good medicine for his wounds. She silently offered a prayer of thanks as she made a poultice of the leaves and packed it onto the cuts.

wapalwaapal

Then she sat back on her heels and drew a deep breath. *We must look out for each other,* she signed. *You and I are not enemies.*

No, we are not enemies, Two Hawks signed.

We have to stay together, she added. *We have to help each other.*

He nodded, his eyes downcast. *You did a good thing for me. How do you say "good" in your language?*

"Tawts!" she said at once.

After a moment, Two Hawks repeated, "Tawts. Tawts, Kaya."

When light came again, Kaya and Two Hawks made their way up the stream, looking for a good place to fish. Kaya's breath clouded at her lips. During the night, a skin of ice had formed along the shore. How much longer would snow hold off?

Here the stream widened into a basin before tumbling farther down. This was a good place to catch trout or mountain whitefish.

Kaya untied a piece of fringe from her skirt to use as a sniggle. She lay on her belly by the pool and dangled the fringe in the water. Fish would think the sniggle was food and bite into it. If she was quick, she could flip the fish onto the bank.

Two Hawks tugged a piece of fringe from the side of his leggings and lay down near her. He dangled the fringe in the water and waited. Almost at once, a fish bit the fringe. Expertly, he flipped a large trout onto the stones.

Soon Kaya felt a tug on her sniggle. With a flick of her wrist, she flipped another trout out of the stream and onto the bank. Good—they had enough for a meal.

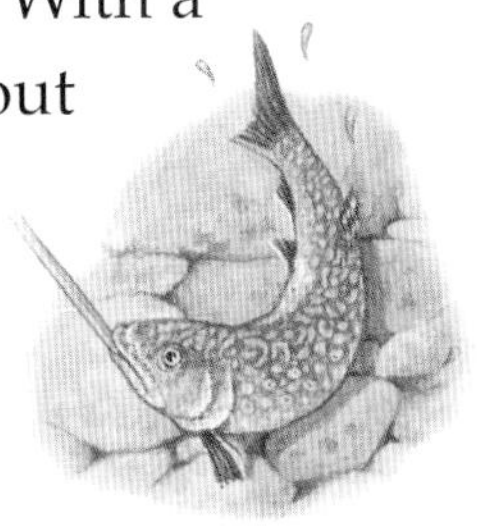

I'll build a fire, Two Hawks signed.

Kaya watched him choose a sharp stick for a fire drill. He put the point of the drill into a hole in a dry branch. Then he rubbed the stick between his palms until tiny sparks fell onto dried moss. Soon a little flame burned, which he carefully fanned into a fire.

Kaya silently thanked the trout for giving themselves to her and the boy for food. Then she cleaned the fish and placed them on sticks by the fire to cook. When the fish were done, she and Two Hawks sat by the fire and ate them. She licked every bit of oil from her fingers. Never had anything tasted more delicious than this meal they'd made together.

As Two Hawks made a fire bundle to save the coals of their fire, a fine, cold rain began to fall. *Hurry!* Kaya signed. They had to find the Buffalo Trail before it was hidden by ice and snow.

As Kaya and Two Hawks made their way uphill, the cold rain turned into sleet. Kaya pulled her deer hide over her head, but the sleet made it hard to see. She thought they'd been following the stream that would lead to the Buffalo Trail, but nothing here looked familiar.

After a time, the stream they followed was nothing more than a small creek racing down the mountainside. Bighorn sheep leaped across ledges

above them. Slipping on icy stones, Kaya and Two Hawks struggled upward. At last they reached the top. Two Hawks gave her a hand, and she climbed up onto a trail that ran along the ridge.

The trail split around fallen trees—a path made by people on foot. Hoofprints were everywhere along it, too. *It's the Buffalo Trail!* she signed to Two Hawks. Her heart lifted—then she felt a stab of loss again. *If only Speaking Rain were with us!* she thought.

Up here the wind was bitterly cold. Kaya and Two Hawks put their heads down and started along the trail. Kaya saw horse droppings and the remains of fires, but the marks weren't fresh ones. With winter coming, travelers had already left the mountains for shelter in the warmer valleys. But Kaya knew enemies used this trail, too. *Keep a lookout!* she signed. How terrible if enemies should catch them now, with home country only a few sleeps away!

Wet and shivering, the two of them worked together to build a small lean-to against a rocky outcropping far off the trail. Because there was no water up here on the ridge, they scooped handfuls of sleet to suck.

If I had a bow and arrow, I could get us food, Two Hawks signed.

But there's hardly any game up this high, Kaya answered. *We'd still have nothing to eat.*

Then she saw that some pines were marked where people had stripped back the bark to get at the soft underlayer. The underlayer was food for both men and horses when they had nothing else to eat.

Here is food, Kaya signed. She began stripping back the bark with her knife.

As Kaya and the boy ate, wolves began to howl to each other across the ridges. Kaya and Two Hawks huddled together for warmth like puppies.

At first light, ice crystals glittered on frozen branches that rattled in the wind. Kaya and Two Hawks lined their moccasins with moss to keep their toes from freezing. Their fingers were blue and their teeth chattered when they took to the trail again, but during the night the sleet had stopped.

Even though she was cold, this old, worn trail comforted Kaya. She felt the presence of the people who had passed this way before her.

After walking a long time, they came to a large cairn, a pile of stones that marked a special place. People had built many cairns along the Buffalo Trail. The cairns marked sacred places where spirits were very strong. Two Hawks went on down the trail to scout their way, but Kaya stopped by the old cairn.

As she stood there, she thought she heard the voices of spirits. Were they reminding her that her name meant "she who arranges rocks"? Were they telling her to build another cairn at this sacred place?

She couldn't lift big stones, so she collected small ones and piled them up until she'd made a mound. She wanted to offer something of her own, too. She opened her bag and looked inside. There was the magpie feather she'd kept. "Magpie," her nickname. She tucked the feather under the top stone of the mound.

All day, and all the next day, they climbed higher and higher. Kaya and Two Hawks looked around as they walked, often glancing up at the birds and clouds for signs of the weather. Suddenly, Two Hawks pointed to a large tree far off the trail. There, high in the tree, was a platform of branches. A bundle was tied onto the platform. Had hunters left food here for their return journey?

Two Hawks climbed up the tree to see. He came down with a rawhide bag slung over his shoulder. The rawhide was from the top part of a tepee, darkened from smoke that made it waterproof. *This is a Salish bundle,* he signed. *My people hunt on this side of the mountain. My people hid this food here!*

Eagerly, they opened the bag. Inside were dried camas cakes and pemmican, a mixture of dried meat, grease, and dried berries. They sat under the tree to eat the tasty, nourishing pemmican. This unexpected find would give them the strength to push on.

They were hurrying up along the trail when Two Hawks signaled for Kaya to halt. *Look,* he signed. *Do you know that country?*

Kaya looked where he pointed. In the far, far distance she could see what seemed to be a stretch of prairie. Was that the prairie where her people sometimes dug camas bulbs? If it was, they were closer to home country than she'd thought. *Soon we will be with my people!* she signed.

Come on! Two Hawks answered. *Let's get a better look!*

Kaya's heart was light as they scrambled up off the trail to a place where they could see more clearly. From up here, the prairie looked like a brown blanket laid over the land. Two Hawks was even more eager than she to see it. He climbed a tall pine until he was almost to the top, leaned out, and shaded his eyes.

With a sharp crack, the branch he stood on snapped under his weight! Crying out with surprise, he pitched backward and fell. He crashed down through the branches. With a thud he hit the rocky ground and tumbled down the hill on the far side. He cried out again, this time in pain.

Kaya rushed down to him. Clutching his ankle, he lay on his side. She crouched and saw a lump on his ankle. When she touched it, he gasped.

She handed him a stick to use as a cane. He seized the stick and tried to rise, but when he put weight on his injured leg, he collapsed in pain. He tried again, only to fall a second time. His face was wet with sweat from his struggle. *My ankle is broken,* he signed.

Kaya bit her lip. She knew she wasn't strong enough to carry Two Hawks more than a little way. Maybe he could crawl a little way, too. But if he couldn't, how would they get out of the mountains?

She hugged herself. What should they do now? The cold wind whipped about them, and last light was coming soon. They needed a shelter and a fire.

Kaya collected dry twigs and sticks and handed Two Hawks the fire bundle he'd made. Grimacing in pain, he unwrapped the coals in the fire bundle and set about building a fire. As he worked, she gathered branches and built a lean-to shelter. How she wished for many, many hides to make the shelter windtight! They had the Salish food, but Two Hawks was in too much pain to eat. His teeth chattered and his whole body shook. His eyes were wide with fright.

How could Kaya help him? She lay down against his back and put her arms around him to keep him as warm as possible. Still, he trembled violently, though he would not cry.

Then Kaya thought of the lullaby that Speaking Rain had sung. Kaya put her lips close to the boy's ear. "*Ha no nee,*" she sang very softly. "*Ha no nee.*" When at last he did sleep, he groaned over and over.

Somehow, Kaya slept, too. She opened her eyes to a white world. Snow was falling thickly. Glittering flakes filled the air and drove into the opening of the lean-to. Snow covered the ground and weighed down the branches of the trees.

Two Hawks tried again to rise, only to collapse onto his side. Kaya knew she couldn't carry him on the steep and icy trail. She'd have to leave him here, hurry on, and try to reach her people. If he stayed in the lean-to with some food, perhaps he wouldn't freeze before she returned with help.

She crawled out of the lean-to and looked up toward the ridge. Drifts and blowing snow were all she could see. By now, snow would have covered the Buffalo Trail as well.

As she stood in the whirling white, she saw a woman standing under a pine tree on the slope. The woman was tall and strong, like the woman named Swan Circling. She wore an elk hide over her shoulders, and snow glistened in her braids. Light surrounded her, like the sun shining on ice. While Kaya watched, the woman turned and strode up toward the ridge, looking back over her shoulder from time to time.

Kaya clutched her hide around herself and followed. Upward she climbed, wet snow falling onto her shoulders from pine branches when she brushed against them. Snow fell onto her head and into her eyes. She wiped her eyes, and when she looked again, the woman was gone. In her place, a wolf stood gazing at Kaya with yellow eyes. She saw the black tips of its raised ears and its thick, yellow-gray coat. It watched her intently as she climbed up to the ridge.

When Kaya reached the top, the wolf trotted slowly down the slope on the other side. It paused now and then and looked back at her, as if waiting for her to come along. Was the wolf a *wyakin?* Kaya hurried after it, and then, with a bound, the wolf leaped down into the trees and disappeared.

"Wait for me!" Kaya whispered. With the wolf gone, the woods seemed much lonelier.

As she searched the hillside for the wolf, she

When Kaya looked again, the woman was gone.
In her place, a wolf stood gazing at her with yellow eyes.

saw something moving. She ducked out of sight behind a tree and peeked around through the veil of snow. Farther down the hillside, she made out a horse and a rider wrapped in a buffalo hide. Enemy? Friend? The rider led a pack horse and rode a large bay stallion. Could it be Runner, her father's horse? Could Toe-ta be here in the mountains?

Kaya went slipping and skidding down the hill, snow flying up around her feet. "Toe-ta!" she cried as she went.

"Kaya!" he called back, and turned the horses uphill to meet her.

Then he was leaning over, lifting her up, putting her onto his horse in front of him. He wrapped her in the warm buffalo robe he wore and held her close. "Daughter, you're alive!" he said. "And Speaking Rain? Is she alive, too?"

Kaya put her face against Toe-ta's chest. It was like a dream to be in his strong arms again.

"Speaking Rain's alive, but she's a slave of our enemies," she said. "I escaped with a Salish boy, but he broke his ankle. He's over that hill!" She pointed.

Toe-ta took fur-lined moccasins from his pack and put them on Kaya's cold feet. He pulled out another buffalo robe, wrapped it around Kaya's shoulders, and set her behind him on Runner. Leading the pack horse, they started back over the ridge to get Two Hawks.

Kaya clung tightly to Toe-ta's back. "How did you find me?" she asked.

"We searched and searched but found nothing," Toe-ta said in his deep voice. "Then two sleeps ago, a scout came to our hunting camp on the Lochsa. He'd come down from the Buffalo Trail to the river because snow was coming. He told us he'd seen a new cairn at a sacred place along the trail. The cairn was made of small stones—ones someone with small hands might choose. Hands like yours, Daughter.

"The scout said a magpie feather was stuck into the little cairn. I thought of your nickname—Magpie. I left our hunting camp and came up here to search for you. But if you hadn't seen me and come running, I wouldn't have found you in this snow. Were you watching the trail?"

"I didn't know where the trail was—" Kaya began, but then she stopped herself. She wouldn't speak of the spirit woman who led her away from the lean-to. She wouldn't speak of the wolf who had brought her in sight of the Buffalo Trail and Toe-ta, either. If the wolf was a wyakin, she would not tell anyone until the proper time came.

So much had happened to Kaya—how could she tell all of it? Where would she start? "Toe-ta, the raiders traded away my horse," she said.

"She's a good horse," he said slowly. "Perhaps you'll see her someday."

"And Two Hawks—can we help him get back to his people?" she asked.

"We'll help the boy join his people when the snow melts and it's time to dig roots again," Toe-ta assured her.

Kaya pressed her face to Toe-ta's back. She closed her eyes tightly and forced herself to say what she had to admit. "It's my fault Speaking Rain's a slave," she whispered. "I thought of my horse before I thought of Speaking Rain's safety. But I made a vow I'd bring her back to us—somehow."

Toe-ta reached back and pulled the buffalo robe closer about Kaya. "We'll do all we can to find Speaking Rain, but you must not blame yourself that you were taken captive," he said. "You were taken far from home, and you've endured much. But,

Daughter, you are alive and well! Let us give thanks to Hun-ya-wat that you're with us again!"

A Peek Into the Past

Learning in 1764

These girls from the early 1900s are building play tepees just as Kaya did. In Kaya's time, play tepees were important practice—women were responsible for building their families' homes.

When Kaya was a girl, her classroom was the world around her, and family members were her teachers. Girls learned from their mothers, grandmothers, aunts, older sisters, and other village women. Boys learned from their male relatives and other men of the village.

By the time a girl was three years old, she would already be helping with daily tasks. She would help the women collect berries and dig roots, using her toy digging stick and baskets to

Girls laced their dolls into toy cradleboards the same way real mothers did.

Kaya knew to steer clear of grizzly bears—they could kill a person with one swipe.

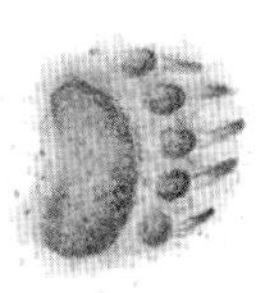

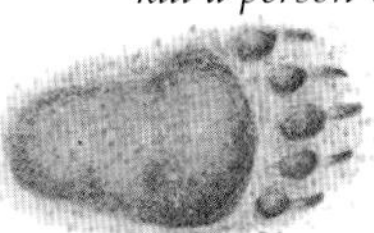

practice gathering food. After age ten, boys accompanied the men on fishing and hunting trips with toy bows and arrows.

By the age of six, boys and girls were already helpers in gathering food. A nine-year-old girl like Kaya would be learning how to cook food and prepare it for winter storage. She would learn how to soften the hides of animals and to make clothes and moccasins from the prepared skins. She would learn how to weave baskets and bags, and she would begin to learn how to help build and furnish a home for her own family one day.

Nez Perce children learned how to recognize—and avoid—the markings of dangerous animals like rattlesnakes and grizzly bears. They learned that swallows signaled the return of the spring salmon and the frogs' song meant that warm weather was on the way. They learned to identify landmarks that showed the way to the best root-digging fields and fishing spots.

Children were taught to be clean and trained to be strong. Every morning—in all seasons—they bathed in a stream, and every evening they cleansed themselves in a sweat lodge. They exercised constantly, running foot races, riding horses, and playing ball games, often with one

Rock cairns were landmarks that marked strong spirit places. Each one had a different meaning, known only to those who built and used them.

Nez Perce saddles had high pommels, or handles, that came in handy for hanging bags on long journeys.

village playing against another. Riding and racing horses was a particularly important skill to Nez Perces, who learned to be comfortable in the saddle as young as three years of age. Girls took part in all these activities and were as skillful as the boys. All these lessons gave children like Kaya the skills they needed to survive in the outdoors.

Grandparents, or elders, were the main teachers in the community because they had the most patience, wisdom, and experience. They taught children like Kaya to have sharp memories. Everything in Nez Perce culture was passed on by example and through songs, stories, and legends that Nez Perces learned by heart. Stories in their complete versions could take days to tell.

Nez Perce children learned about their history and customs through these legends. The tales showed how Nez Perces could be guided by spiritual powers, and they emphasized justice, bravery, independence, and generosity. In the story of *Ant and Yellow Jacket*, Nez Perce children learned that if you are greedy for more than your share, you may lose everything.

Nez Perces prided themselves on remembering all that was important. Elders remembered the names of hundreds of family members and could create elaborate patterns and symbols completely from memory.

Ant & Yellow Jacket

In the old days, the Yellow Jackets and the Ants all lived together on the hillside. One day, while Chief Yellow Jacket was eating his favorite meal on his favorite rock, Chief Ant came by. He became angry that Chief Yellow Jacket was using that rock.

"Hey there, Yellow Jacket," Chief Ant shouted. "What are you doing on that rock? I have as much right to sit there as you do!"

Chief Yellow Jacket looked up in surprise. "What are you shouting about, Ant? You know I always eat my dinner here." The two chiefs started fighting.

About that time, Coyote passed by.

"Stop fighting!" Coyote ordered. "There's plenty of room and food for all of us."

The chiefs kept fighting. Finally, Coyote warned them to stop or he would turn them to stone. Still they didn't stop. They reared up with backs arched, gripping one another around the neck. At that moment, Coyote waved his paws and turned them to stone.

The Nez Perces' form of education served them well for thousands of years. But during the 1800s, their traditional way of life was changing. By the late 1800s, the United States government had begun confining Indians across the country to tracts of land called reservations. At the same time, the government leaders decided to educate Indians in the ways of the white people. Government leaders believed that Indians would be better off if they forgot their traditional ways. The easiest way to do this, government officials realized, was to send Indian children to boarding schools, away from family members who still practiced traditional customs.

A Nez Perce girl dressed for boarding school

Government officials forced Nez Perces to send their children to the Indian School at Lapwai (near the Nez Perce Reservation), Chemawa Indian School in Oregon, or Carlisle Indian School in Pennsylvania. Students had to wear non-Indian clothes and eat unfamiliar foods. They were expected to learn English and were punished—even beaten—if caught using their native languages. For Indian children, who had always lived among extended family, it was

Nez Perce girls in cooking class

a shocking and lonely experience to be taken away from home. Many children couldn't eat or sleep. Others became depressed or sick. Some died.

As a result of boarding schools, family ties and traditional customs suffered, and few people today can speak the Nez Perce language fluently. Luckily, Nez Perce children today are encouraged to learn about their history and culture. The Nez Perce Tribe, the Colville Confederated Tribes of Washington, and the Confederated Tribes of the Umatilla sponsor Nez Perce language classes for children and adults.

At school, camp, and home, Nez Perce boys and girls learn the same math, science, reading, and other basic lessons taught in schools across America. But they also learn traditional crafts, hear legends and stories, and practice drumming and dancing in traditional clothing. They welcome new ways of learning today while still holding on to what is precious from their past.

Nez Perce children today learn traditional skills such as weaving baskets and how to speak the Nez Perce language in their classrooms.

Glossary of Nez Perce Words

In the story, Nez Perce words are spelled so that English readers can pronounce them. Here, you can also see how the words are actually spelled and said by the Nez Perce people.

Phonetic/Nez Perce	Pronunciation	Meaning
aa-heh/'éehe	*AA-heh*	yes, that's right
Eetsa/Iice	*EET-sah*	Mother
Hun-ya-wat/ Hanyaw'áat	*hun-yah-WAHT*	the Creator
Kautsa/Qaaca'c	*KOUT-sah*	grandmother from mother's side
Kaya'aton'my'	*ky-YAAH-a-ton-my*	she who arranges rocks
Nimíipuu	*Nee-MEE-poo*	The People; known today as the Nez Perce Indians
Salish/Sélix	*SAY-leesh*	friends of the Nez Perce who live near them
tawts/ta'c	*TAWTS*	good
Toe-ta/Toot'a	*TOH-tah*	Father
Wallowa/ Wal'áwa	*wah-LAU-wa*	Wallowa Valley in present-day Oregon
wapalwaapal	*WAH-pul-WAAH-pul*	western yarrow, a plant that helps stop bleeding
wyakin/ wéeyekin	*WHY-ah-kin*	guardian spirit

The Books About Kaya

Meet Kaya • An American Girl
Kaya's boasting gets her into big trouble and earns her a terrible nickname.

Kaya's Escape! • A Survival Story
Kaya and her sister, Speaking Rain, are captured in an enemy raid. Can they find a way to escape?

Kaya's Hero • A Story of Giving
Kaya becomes close friends with a warrior woman named Swan Circling, who inspires Kaya and gives her an amazing gift.

Kaya and Lone Dog • A Friendship Story
Kaya befriends a lone dog, who teaches her about love and letting go.

Kaya Shows the Way • A Sister Story
Kaya is reunited with Speaking Rain, who has a surprising decision to share.

Changes for Kaya • A Story of Courage
Kaya and her horse, Steps High, are caught in a flash fire. Can they outrun it?

Coming in Spring 2003
Welcome to Kaya's World • 1764
History is lavishly illustrated with photographs, paintings, and artifacts of the Nez Perce people.